CLASSIC COLLECTION

ANNE OF GREEN GABLES

LUCY MAUD MONTGOMERY

ADAPTED BY ANNE ROONEY · ILLUSTRATED BY CATHARINE COLLINGRIDGE

A Surprise at Green Gables

Mrs Rachel Lynde was most surprised to see Matthew Cuthbert driving his buggy up the hill, dressed smartly, at half-past three on a sunny afternoon. He should have been at home planting his turnip seed.

Rachel Lynde felt it her business to know everything that went on in Avonlea. "I'll just step over to Green Gables and find out from Marilla where her brother's gone," she said to herself.

Rachel noted immediately that Marilla's table was set with three places – so Matthew must be bringing someone back. The tea was not fancy, so it could not be for a very grand visitor.

"We're getting a little orphan boy from Nova Scotia," Marilla told her. "Matthew went to Bright River to collect him." Matthew was getting older and an orphan boy could help him with chores.

Rachel could not have been more surprised if Marilla had said they were getting a kangaroo from Australia! The world was turning upside down. Rachel always spoke her mind, and told Marilla that she thought it a mighty foolish thing to do. An unknown child might burn the house down, or poison the wells! Rachel hurried off to spread the news – she loved to cause a sensation. She did feel sorry for the orphan, though. A child at Green Gables! But Rachel would have felt even sorrier if she could have seen the child waiting patiently on the railway platform.

When Matthew arrived at the station there was no one there but a little girl, sitting on the platform. He asked when the train was expected.

"It's been and gone," the stationmaster said. "There was a passenger dropped off for you – a little girl."

"But I've come to collect a boy," Matthew said.

"Maybe they ran out of boys," the stationmaster said.

Matthew didn't like talking much, and talking to a strange little girl seemed like the hardest thing! The girl was about eleven. She had long red hair in two plaits, big green eyes, and her pale face was covered with freckles. She wore an ugly dress that was too short.

"I suppose you are Mr Matthew Cuthbert?" she said. "I thought perhaps you wouldn't come. If you hadn't come, I would have slept in a tree, because you would surely come tomorrow."

The girl talked on and on through their long ride to Green Gables.

"Doesn't that white tree make you think of a bride? I should love a white dress, though I will never marry because I am too plain. I've never had a pretty dress, but I can imagine one. Don't you love to imagine things?"

"Well, I don't know that I do," Matthew answered.

"Is there a brook at Green Gables? I have always dreamed of living near a stream. Wouldn't it be nice if dreams came true?"

Matthew decided Marilla could tell the girl that she wasn't wanted.

Marilla's Decision

"Who's that?" Marilla said, looking at the little girl. "Where's the boy?"

"There isn't one," Matthew said.

"But we asked for a boy!" Marilla said.

"You don't want me because I'm not a boy!" Anne cried. Marilla tried to calm her, but she would not be calmed.

"You would cry if you were an orphan and thought you'd found a home, and then weren't wanted because you're not a boy!" she sobbed.

Marilla started to smile. She asked the girl's name.

"It is Anne Shirley – Anne with an 'e'," she said.

Marilla said Anne could stay until morning, and showed her to the little room under the east gable. It was bare and white. Anne shivered as she looked around it.

"She'll have to go back," Marilla said later that evening.

"I suppose so," Matthew said, sadly.

"What do you mean, you 'suppose so'? You can't want to keep her? What use would she be to us?"

"We might be some use to her," Matthew suggested.

"I'm not keeping her," Marilla said, firmly.

The next day, Anne gazed in wonder out of the window.

"Isn't it all so lovely?" she said when Marilla came in. "The orchard, and the brook and the flowers. What's that geranium called? I shall call it Bonny. I like things to have names."

"I never saw anything like her," Marilla muttered to herself. "She is kind of interesting."

After lunch Marilla took Anne to the White Sands village to sort out the mix-up. On the way, Anne told Marilla how her parents had died when she was a baby. She'd been sent to live with various people, but had ended up in the orphanage. Marilla felt sorry for her.

When they got to White Sands, Mrs Spencer, who had organized Anne's arrival, said it wasn't her fault that they'd been sent a girl. Mrs Blewett, who was just coming up the path, said she wanted to adopt a girl, though. Mrs Blewett looked sharply at Anne.

"There's not much to you. You'll have to earn your keep," she said sourly.

The misery on Anne's face softened Marilla's heart.

"I haven't decided definitely," Marilla said. "Matthew is rather fond of her. I must ask him first."

Anne could hardly believe it, she was so happy. And so was Matthew when they got home.

"I wouldn't give a dog to that Blewett woman," he said to Marilla when they were alone.

"I've never brought up a child," Marilla said, "especially not a girl. I expect I'll make a dreadful mess of it – but I'll give it a go if I must."

Marilla didn't tell Anne immediately.

"Please, Marilla," Anne begged, the next day, "won't you tell me if you're going to send me away?"

"Matthew and I have decided to keep you – if you will be good," Marilla said, as sternly as she could manage.

Anne burst into happy tears.

Mrs Lynde is Horrified

Anne had been at Green Gables for two weeks when Mrs Lynde next visited. She would have come earlier, but had been ill with flu. Anne spent most of those weeks outside, making friends with the trees and flowers and the brook. She spent the rest of the time chattering about them until Matthew and Marilla felt half-deafened. Matthew listened to all of it, but Marilla was less patient and silenced Anne.

"I'm very surprised at you and Matthew," Mrs Lynde said. "Couldn't you have sent her back?"

"I admit I'm beginning to like her," said Marilla.

"She's terribly skinny, Marilla," Mrs Lynde said. "Look at her freckles! And that hair is as red as carrots!"

Furiously, Anne shouted at her: "I hate you! How dare you say I'm skinny and have carrot hair? How would you like it if people said you were fat and clumsy?"

The two women stared in horror, then Marilla sent Anne straight to her room. Marilla started to apologize to Mrs Lynde, but instead found herself saying, "You were harsh. You shouldn't have criticized her looks."

"Well, I had better be careful what I say around here," said Mrs Lynde sharply, "to make sure I don't offend any poor orphans. I hope you will beat her for that, Marilla!" And, with that, Mrs Rachel Lynde stormed off home.

Marilla found Anne crying on her bed. She told her off, and said that she must stay in her room until she was ready to apologize to Mrs Lynde.

"Then I must stay here forever," Anne replied. "I can't say sorry to her as I'm not sorry."

For the whole of the next day, Marilla took Anne's meals upstairs on a tray. Finally, Matthew crept shyly up to Anne's room.

"You'll have to do it sooner or later," he said.

"I suppose I could now," Anne replied. "For you. I couldn't before as I was too cross."

"But don't say I persuaded you," Matthew pleaded.

Anne called Marilla later and told her she was ready to apologize. The next morning they set off.

Anne knelt before Mrs Lynde.

"Oh, Mrs Lynde," she said. "I am so very sorry. You can't imagine how sorry I am! I'm so dreadfully wicked and should be punished."

Anne went on so much that Marilla felt sure she was enjoying it. At last, Mrs Lynde told her to get up. She even said that as Anne grew older, her hair might turn auburn instead of red.

When they got home, Marilla told Anne not to think about her looks so much as it was very vain.

"How can it be vain, when I know I am not pretty?" Anne asked. "It upsets me that I am not pretty."

But Anne soon put the unfortunate episode behind her and began to settle into her life at Green Gables.

Meeting Diana

Marilla had made Anne three new dresses, but they were very plain.

"How do you like them?" she asked.

"I shall pretend to like them," Anne replied. "But I'd like them a good deal better if they had puffed sleeves. Everyone else has puffed sleeves."

"Such concerns are utter nonsense!" cried Marilla.

On Sunday, Anne went to Sunday school. On her return Marilla asked her about it.

"Everyone else had puffed sleeves," she replied. "And Miss Rogerson asked too many questions, and Mr Bell's prayer was dull, and the sermon was too long."

Marilla thought she should tell her off, but secretly she agreed about the sermon. But when she heard that Anne had decorated her hat with flowers on the way to church, she did tell her off. Anne was upset and afraid that Marilla would send her back to the orphanage.

"I don't want to send you back – I just don't want you to look ridiculous! Now, Mrs Barry's little girl Diana came back today. Do you want to come and meet her?"

Anne was trembling with excitement. She desperately hoped that Diana would become her best friend.

When they got to the Barry's house, she found Diana was a pretty girl with dark hair and eyes. They went outside to play together. Diana was everything Anne had hoped for, and they swore an oath to be best friends.

A Picnic

One August evening, Anne ran home bursting with excitement.

"Oh, Marilla!" she cried. "There's to be a Sunday school picnic next week with ice cream! May I go, please?"

"Of course you may," Marilla answered.

On Sunday, Marilla had worn her best brooch to church. But, on Monday evening, Marilla couldn't find it anywhere. Anne said she'd tried it on, but had put it back. Marilla looked everywhere. In the end, she decided Anne was lying. But Anne would not confess, even when Marilla said she must stay in her room until she did.

"But the picnic is tomorrow," Anne cried.

"You'll not go until you've confessed," Marilla insisted.

When Marilla took up breakfast the next day, Anne said she'd accidentally dropped the brooch into the stream.

"Can you give me my punishment quickly so that I can go to the picnic?" she asked.

"No picnic," Marilla said. "That's your punishment!" She left Anne sobbing on her bed.

But that afternoon, Marilla noticed something gleaming in her shawl – the lost brooch! She went to Anne's room.

"The only way to get to the picnic was to confess," Anne said, "so I had to."

"Well, we'd better get you to that picnic!" Marilla said.

And that night, after the picnic, a tired Anne returned to Green Gables in a state of such happiness, that she was lost for words.

A Bad Start

The summer ended and Anne started school in Avonlea. Marilla was worried, but the first day Anne came home full of chatter. A few days later, the handsome Gilbert Blythe tried to attract Anne's attention. Anne had no interest in boys, which was something Gilbert was not used to.

"Carrots!" he called to her. Furious, Anne raised her writing slate and cracked it over his head. She got into dreadful trouble! Gilbert told the teacher, Mr Philips, that it was his own fault for teasing her, but Anne still had to stand by the blackboard for the rest of the lesson.

Gilbert tried to make peace with Anne on the way home, but she walked straight past him. Things got even worse the next day, when Mr Philips punished Anne for being late back from lunch by making her sit beside Gilbert. The others were late, too, but only Anne was punished. At the end of the day, Anne packed up everything in her desk and took it with her.

"What are you doing?" Diana asked.

"I am never going back to that school," she said. "I shall learn all my lessons at home."

Marilla wasn't impressed, but when she saw there was no arguing with Anne, she went to talk to Rachel Lynde. Rachel loved to give advice.

"Let her stay at home," she said. "She'll cool off in a week or so and go back of her own free will."

Raspberry Cordial

One beautiful day in October, Marilla was going out and told Anne she could invite Diana over for tea. They could have tea and cakes, cherry jam and the last of the raspberry cordial in the pantry.

When the afternoon came, the two girls sat in the orchard and discussed the news from school. As soon as Diana mentioned Gilbert Blythe, though, Anne suggested they go in and have some raspberry cordial – she didn't want to hear anything about him.

She found the bottle on the top shelf of the pantry.

"That's the nicest raspberry cordial I've ever tasted," said Diana, and she drank three large glasses.

Anne didn't have any, but gossiped on and on. After a while, Diana stood up unsteadily.

"I feel awfully sick," she said. "I must go home immediately." Nothing Anne could say would persuade her to stay.

On Monday, Marilla sent Anne to Mrs Lynde's on an errand. She returned in floods of tears.

"Whatever has gone wrong now?" asked Marilla.

"Mrs Barry told Mrs Lynde I sent Diana home drunk! And that she will never let Diana see me again!"

Marilla went to investigate. She found it hard not to laugh when she realized that she'd put the raspberry cordial in the cellar and the bottle Anne had found was currant wine. First Marilla, and then Anne, went to Mrs Barry to explain and apologize, but it was no use.

"I don't think you're a suitable friend for Diana at all," Mrs Barry said sharply, and shut the door. Anne fled back to Green Gables and cried herself to sleep.

The next afternoon, Diana arrived at Green Gables. Her mother had allowed her only ten minutes to say a final goodbye to Anne. They exchanged locks of hair and Anne thought she would die of grief.

But, on Monday, she had an idea. She decided to go back to school – then at least she could see Diana. Marilla was pleased and Anne was welcomed back by everyone, even by Gilbert, who she ignored.

Anne decided to be a model pupil, and was soon coming top of the class. Only Gilbert Blythe could compete with her, and a strong rivalry developed.

One night in January, when Marilla was out and Anne was at home with Matthew, Diana came to Green Gables in a terrible panic.

"Anne, come quick! My little sister, Minnie May, is terribly sick and Mother and Father are out. I'm so scared!"

Matthew went to find a doctor while Anne and Diana went back to the Barry house. Anne had helped to look after small children in the orphanage and knew what medicine to take with her. For hours, she looked after Minnie May, and when the doctor finally came, he said Anne had saved the child's life. The next day, Mrs Barry said she was so grateful that Anne could see Diana again after all.

A Shock in the Night

One evening in February, Diana invited Anne to go to a concert and to stay overnight with her. When they got back, they were still excited.

"Let's race to the spare room and jump on the bed," Anne suggested. She ran down the corridor and flew through the air, landing in the middle of the bed.

"Oh, goodness!" cried a voice from under the covers.

"What was that?" gasped Anne, in fright.

Diana's old aunt, Miss Josephine Barry, was not at all happy at being jumped on in the night. She complained to Diana's mother and said she would not let Diana have the music lessons she had promised her.

Anne went to the old lady's room in the morning and apologized as best she could.

"Do you know what it's like to be jumped on in the night?" Miss Barry said crossly.

"No, I don't," said Anne, "but I can truly imagine. And can you imagine, Miss Barry, what it's like to be a little orphan girl who has never had the honour of sleeping in a spare room?"

Miss Barry laughed. "Why don't you stay and talk to me for a while?" she asked.

"I can't," Anne replied. "I have to go back to Marilla, who is the kind lady who is trying to bring me up properly. It is discouraging work."

Over the coming months, Anne often visited Miss Barry and they became firm friends.

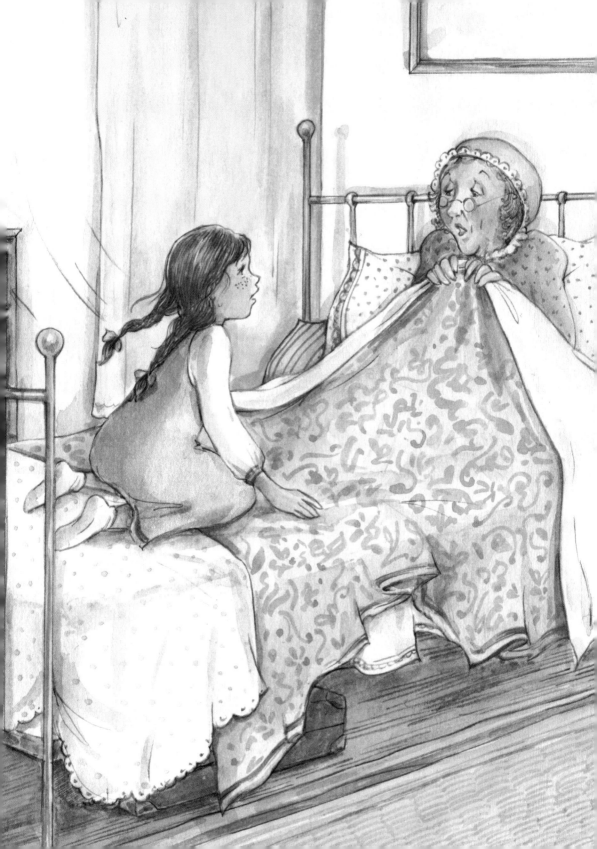

Anne's Accident

Spring came and went and, in late June, both Mr Philips and the minister left. A new minister, called Mr Allan, arrived with his young wife, and Marilla invited them to tea. She asked Anne to make a cake.

Although Anne was worried about her cake, it rose beautifully and she looked forward to the minister's wife enjoying it. But Mrs Allan took one bite of the cake and gave a very strange look. Marilla tried it.

"What on earth did you put in this cake, child?" she cried. "It's simply horrible!"

Anne said she had used vanilla and brought the bottle labelled, 'Best Vanilla'. Marilla smelled it.

"Goodness, it's muscle ointment!" she cried. "I broke the ointment bottle last week and poured what was left into an old vanilla bottle. Why couldn't you smell it?"

Anne fled to her room and flung herself on the bed.

Soon after, the door opened, but Anne was still lying face down on the bed, crying.

"Marilla, I'm disgraced forever!" she sobbed. "Mrs Allan will think I tried to poison her! Though ointment is not poisonous. Please won't you tell her?"

"Why don't you tell her yourself?" said a voice. Anne looked up to see Mrs Allan in her room.

"Don't cry," Mrs Allan said. "It was just a funny mistake anyone could have made."

"It takes me to make a mistake like that," Anne said sadly.

Two weeks later, Mrs Allan invited Anne to tea at the manse house, where she lived with the minister. Anne had a wonderful time, and learned that their new teacher was a woman. She could hardly wait for school to start.

A little before the new term started, Diana Barry had a party. After tea, the girls began a game of 'dare'. Anne dared Josie Pye to walk along the top of the fence. Josie did it well and Anne tossed her red plaits defiantly.

"That's not hard," she said. "I knew a girl who could walk the ridgepole on the roof of her house."

It was a foolish thing to say, for Josie dared Anne to do just that – and Anne was too proud to refuse. All the girls held their breath as Anne climbed up and walked the ridgepole. After just a few steps, she swayed and crashed to the ground, where she lay white and limp.

"Anne, are you killed?" shrieked Diana.

"I'm not killed, but I think I'm unconscious," Anne answered. Just then, a horrified Mrs Barry came out. The doctor came, and said Anne's ankle was broken.

It took a while for the ankle to heal and Anne had to start school late, but she immediately loved Miss Stacy, the new teacher.

"She wants me to recite poetry at her next concert!" Anne told Marilla excitedly one evening.

"That's just filling your head with nonsense," Marilla sniffed. "I don't like children giving concerts. It makes them fond of showing off."

A Dress from Matthew

One day in December, Matthew decided to buy Anne a nice dress, without telling Marilla. He asked Mrs Lynde to help, and she produced a fancy brown dress with puffed sleeves. When Matthew gave it to Anne, at Christmas, she burst into tears.

"Don't you like it?" Matthew asked.

"Oh, Matthew, it's perfect!" she answered.

Anne wore the dress to Miss Stacy's concert where she gave a beautiful recital and was the star of the show.

The winter months passed uneventfully until Marilla came home one evening expecting Anne to have laid tea. But the house was empty. She grew cross. At last, she went upstairs with a candle, and found the girl hiding.

"Please, Marilla, don't look at me!" Anne said. But, of course, Marilla did look, and found that Anne's hair was bright green!

"I thought nothing could be as bad as red hair, so I dyed it," Anne sobbed. "But I was wrong. I wanted it to be black but it's gone green!"

"You dyed it!" Marilla cried. "Didn't you know that was a wicked thing to do?"

No amount of washing removed the green dye. Marilla had to cut off all of Anne's hair, as short as possible. Of course, everyone at school made a terrible fuss. Josie Pye said she looked like a scarecrow, but Anne told no one the real reason for her terrible haircut.

A Last Chance

One day, after studying 'The Lady of Shalott' at school, Anne, Diana, Jane and Ruby Gillis decided to act out the love story of Elaine and Sir Lancelot. They went to the pond and laid a shawl in the bottom of a boat. Anne lay in the boat, pretending to be dead. The others pushed her off into the current and raced to the point where they would greet 'Elaine'.

Anne enjoyed the drama – until the boat started to leak. Soon, water was pouring through a big crack in the bottom. Anne was frightened and began to pray hard. For once, her prayers seemed to be answered as the boat swung by a stake which she managed to grab.

The boat sank quickly. The girls waiting at the bridge saw it disappear and began to shriek but, assuming Anne was dead, did not run for help.

Anne found it harder and harder to hold on. But, just as she thought she must let go, Gilbert Blythe rowed under the bridge and saved her. On dry land, she thanked him politely.

"Can't we be friends now?" Gilbert asked. Anne wanted to say yes, but could not forget his old insults.

"No," she said. "I shall never be friends with you."

"Then I won't ask you ever again," he said. As he rowed away, Anne rather wished she had given a different answer. But, when she met the other girls and they said how romantic it was that he rescued her, her heart hardened against Gilbert again.

The Class for Queen's College

On a dull November evening, Marilla laid aside her knitting as her eyes hurt. Recently, they had begun to grow tired easily. She looked tenderly at Anne sitting on the rug and thought how strange it was that she had come to love the girl so dearly.

At last, she said, "Miss Stacy was here this afternoon to talk about you. She came to say she will teach a class of her best students to study for the entrance exam to Queen's College. And she wants you to be in it."

Throughout the winter, they all studied hard, and Anne's rivalry with Gilbert Blythe become open and well-known. But no one knew, not even Diana, how Anne regretted being so harsh when he had saved her.

Summer came, then autumn, and the winter flew by with Anne absorbed in her studies and her rivalry with Gilbert Blythe. Marilla was astonished one day to notice that Anne had grown taller than her. It made her sad to realize that one day Anne would be gone.

The time for the entrance exam came, and Anne felt she had passed, but the three weeks they waited for the results seemed to crawl by. Then one evening, Diana came running through the trees holding a newspaper.

"You've passed!" Diana cried to her. "And you came joint first with Gilbert Blythe!"

They ran to the barn so Anne could tell Matthew.

"Well, now, I always said you could beat them easily!" Matthew said proudly.

The Hotel Concert

Soon afterwards, Anne and Diana sat together in the east gable room choosing Anne's dress for a concert at a hotel in White Sands where Anne was to recite a poem. The room was different from the bare place it had been when Anne first arrived. Now, it was adorned with all the pretty ornaments of a young woman's room.

Anne was not nervous, as she had become used to reciting in public. But when the performer before her turned out to be a professional who recited beautifully, Anne lost her nerve. She thought she would not be able to go on stage at all, and was on the point of backing out when her name was called. But then she saw Gilbert Blythe in the audience. Fear that he would laugh at her spurred her on. She rose to her feet and performed brilliantly – so brilliantly, indeed, that the professional congratulated her.

The three weeks after the concert were spent preparing for Anne's departure to Queen's College. Marilla had a beautiful, frilled, light green dress made for her. Anne was so delighted she put it on and gave them a recital of a poem called 'The Maiden's Vow'. Marilla's eyes filled with tears.

"I was thinking of the little girl you were," she explained, "and wishing you could have stayed a little girl. But you are grown up and going away."

"I'm just the same really," said Anne. "I promise I'll come back soon."

Queen's College and Back

The day came when Matthew drove Anne to town to start at Queen's. She was glad that so many of her former schoolmates were there, too, but missed Diana desperately. Still, her homesickness faded, and she continued her old rivalry with Gilbert Blythe, who had also started at Queen's. There was the gold medal to compete for, and an Avery scholarship to Redmond College. Anne worked hard to make Matthew proud.

She noticed that Gilbert Blythe spent a lot of time with Ruby Gillis, and regretted not forgiving him.

The first year passed quickly and, when the exam came around at the end of the year, Anne was anxious. She thought she would not be able bear it if Gilbert Blythe won the medal, and Emily Clay was expected to win the scholarship. When she reached the hall where the announcements were posted, a crowd was already carrying Gilbert on their shoulders, calling, "Hurrah for Blythe, winner of the medal!"

Anne felt sick – she had failed and Gilbert had won! But, a moment later, another shout went up: "Three cheers for Anne Shirley, winner of the scholarship!" Anne's friends crowded around, congratulating her.

Anne went home to Green Gables in triumph, and her future seemed happily mapped out. Though when she took up her scholarship, she would miss her rivalry with Gilbert – he was staying in Avonlea to teach.

The day after her return to Green Gables, Anne noticed that Matthew didn't look well.

"He's had some bad spells with his heart," Marilla said. "Maybe he'll be better now – you cheer him up."

"You don't look well, either," Anne said.

"It's my eyes," Marilla answered. "I'm going to see the eye doctor. And I'm worried – Mrs Lynde says the Abbey Bank might fail. They have all our money."

Anne spent a happy first day back in her old home, enjoying the countryside. But the next day was very different. She came downstairs to find Marilla crying in alarm, "Matthew! What's wrong? Are you sick?"

He was clutching a newspaper and standing in the doorway. He looked deathly pale. Within a moment, he collapsed to the floor. By the time Mrs Lynde and the doctor arrived, he was dead.

The doctor said his heart had stopped – a shock must have killed him. And the paper in Matthew's hand revealed the Abbey Bank had indeed failed.

The days passed, and Matthew was buried. Anne was devastated and felt guilty at finding pleasure in anything. During a visit to the manse house, Mrs Allen told Anne that Matthew had enjoyed her laughter and would want it to continue.

"I must go home now," Anne said, as it grew dark. "Marilla gets lonely in the evenings."

"She will be even lonelier when you go away to college again," remarked Mrs Allan.

A Change of Plan

When Anne got back to Green Gables that evening, Marilla told her she had seen Gilbert Blythe at church. She thought that Gilbert was a good-looking boy and said he reminded her of his father, John Blythe. Marilla confessed that she had been fond of John when they were young, but they had had a quarrel and she could not forgive him. Afterwards, she had always wished she had given him a second chance, but it was too late, and Marilla had never married. It made Anne think about how she had treated Gilbert.

The next day, Anne found Marilla sitting sadly in the kitchen. She had been to see the eye specialist. He had told her that if she was very careful and wore the glasses he gave her, her eyes might not get worse. But otherwise she would be blind within six months. Anne consoled her as best she could, but it was no use.

Things became even worse a few days later when Anne found Marilla with tears in her eyes.

"I must sell Green Gables," she explained to Anne.

"But you can't sell it!" Anne cried.

Marilla said that with her worsening sight, and Matthew gone, she couldn't run the place alone.

"You won't be alone," Anne said. "I'm not going away. I will stay here with you and teach!"

"Oh, Anne! You can't sacrifice yourself!"

"My mind's made up," said Anne. "It's no sacrifice but rather a pleasure."

Gilbert Blythe

The news soon spread that Anne wasn't going back to college, but would stay and look for a job as a teacher. Those who were unaware of Marilla's eye problems thought Anne was foolish, and there was a great deal of discussion about it. Mrs Allen did not agree. She told Anne, in such kind words that brought tears to Anne's eyes, that she was doing the right thing. A few days later, Mrs Lynde came to visit. She also approved of Anne's decision and told her that the school trustees had decided to give her a job in the school in Avonlea.

"But Gilbert Blythe is taking the job in Avonlea school," Anne said.

"No, he isn't," Rachel replied. "When he heard that you intended to stay here with Marilla, he turned it down and took a job at another school in White Sands."

"I don't feel I ought to take it," said Anne, quietly.

"He's already signed the papers with the other school," said Mrs Lynde. "So you may as well take it."

The next evening, Anne went to lay flowers on Matthew's grave.

"Dear old world," she said to herself, as she walked. "You are very lovely and I am glad to be alive in you."

On her way back down the hill, Anne met Gilbert Blythe. He stopped whistling when he saw her and would have passed in silence, but Anne raised her hand to shake his.

"Gilbert, I want to thank you for giving up the school for me," she said. "It was very good of you and I want you to know I am grateful."

Gilbert nodded eagerly. "I wanted to help you a little," he said. "Do you think we can be friends after this? Can you forgive me for my old insult?"

Anne said that she could, that she was sorry for being so stubborn, and they would both study from home and help each other.

"We are going to be the best of friends," said Gilbert happily. "We were born to be good friends, Anne. Come, I will walk you home."

When Anne got home, Marilla asked her who she had spent such a long time talking to at the gate.

"Gilbert Blythe," said Anne, blushing a little. "I met him coming down the hill."

Anne told Marilla she had made up with Gilbert and they were to be friends. Then she went to her east gable and sat in the window looking out at the familiar scene. The wind purred softly in the cherry trees and the smell of mint reached her nose. Anne felt content. Things had changed so much for her since she had come home from college, but she knew that whatever life now held for her, she would feel happy.

"God's in His heaven, and all's right with the world," she whispered to herself.

About the author

Lucy Maud Montgomery was born on Prince Edward Island, Canada, in 1874. After her mother died, she was brought up by her strict maternal grandparents and had a lonely childhood. Maud, as she was known, developed an active imagination and began to write at a young age. She trained to be a teacher and, in 1908, her first novel, *Anne of Green Gables*, became an instant success. She followed this with a whole series of novels about Anne, which are semi-autobiographical and contain many of her own childhood memories. Her books have been published in over 40 languages and are known all over the world. Lucy Maud Montgomery died in Toronto, Canada in 1942.

Other titles in the Classic Collection series:

The Adventures of Tom Sawyer • *Alice's Adventures in Wonderland*
Black Beauty • *Gulliver's Travels* • *Heidi* • *A Little Princess*
Little Women • *Pinocchio* • *Robin Hood* • *Robinson Crusoe*
The Secret Garden • *The Three Musketeers* • *Treasure Island*
The Wizard of Oz • *20,000 Leagues Under The Sea*

Editor: Louise John • Designer: Rachel Clark
Copyright © QED Publishing 2013

First published in the UK in 2013 by
QED Publishing, A Quarto Group company,
230 City Road, London EC1V 2TT
www.qed-publishing.co.uk

A catalogue record for this book is available from the British Library.

ISBN 978 1 78171 115 6

Printed in China